MAYBELLE
THE
CABLE CAR

BY
VIRGINIA LEE BURTON
HOUGHTON MIFFLIN CO.

www.hmhco.com

Library of Congress Catalog Card Number: 96-9845
RNF ISBN 0-395-82847-3   PAP ISBN 0-395-84003-1
Printed in China
SCP 20 19 18 17
4500670738

Way out in the far Far West
there is a city of many hills...
a city with water on three sides round...
a bay city...a sea port...a gay city...a friendly city...
a city of flowers and cable cars
THE CITY OF SAN FRANCISCO.
To
the people of this city
who love their cable cars and
especially to MRS. HANS KLUSSMAN, leading light
in the fight to save them from extinction,
I dedicate this book

Foreword

The first of the cable cars was born in San Francisco August 1, 1873 . . . the invention of Andrew S. Hallidie. Born because Hallidie was fond of animals and could not bear to see the poor horses struggling and falling down when they tried to climb the steep hills which were so slippery when wet. So successful was the first cable car that soon there were many more . . . as many as eight different companies were formed and operated in San Francisco in the days before the earthquake and fire of 1906.

After the fire many of the cable lines were converted to electricity. Then as the city grew and changed

MUNICIPAL RAILWAY

PRESENT CALIFORNIA ST. CABLE R.R. CO.

OMNIBUS CABLE CO.

"Progress" in the form of streetcars, gasoline buses and trackless trolleys took over all but two of the remaining cable companies — The Municipal Railway Company, owned by the city, and the California Street Cable Railroad Company recently acquired by the city. For lack of space and to simplify matters I have used only the Municipal cable car, but the story of their survival is much the same.

For further information on cable car history I recommend *Cable Car Carnival* by Lucius Beebe and Charles Clegg, and if you want to know what makes them go read Frank Parker's *Anatomy of the San Francisco Cable Car.*

SUTTER ST. RAILROAD CO.

MARKET ST. RAILROAD CO.

Maybelle was a cable car
   a San Francisco cable car
      Cling clang...clingety clang
         Up and down and around she went.

GRIP AND LEVER — CABLE

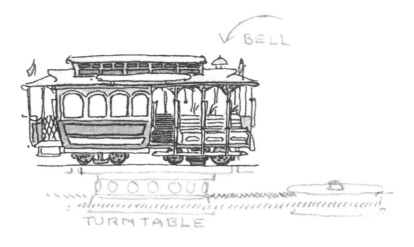

BELL

TURN TABLE

TRACK BRAKE AND LEVER

Maybelle had a bell on top
Ring two to go ... and one to stop.
Underneath she had a grip
to grab the cable under the street.

She had three different kinds of brakes
one for the wheels ... one for the track ...
and an emergency brake to jam in the slot
so she could stop whenever she ought.

FRONT WHEEL BRAKES AND PEDAL
REAR WHEEL BRAKES AND LEVER

EMERGENCY BRAKE AND LEVER

SLOT

GRIP
CHANNEL UNDER STREET

ENDLESS CABLE MOVES
9 MILES AN HOUR

TING TING
GRIPMAN PULLING GRIP LEVER

Maybelle had a Gripman and a Conductor.
The Gripman pulled the levers
pushed the pedal and rang the bell
for Maybelle to stop or go.

The Conductor collected the fares
called out the streets and
helped with the rear wheel brakes
when the hills were very steep.

TING
GRIPMAN PULLING TRACK BRAKE LEVER

TING TING
CONDUCTOR WORKING REAR WHEEL
BRAKES & GRIPMAN PUSHING FOOT
PEDAL FOR FRONT WHEEL BRAKES.

TING
GRIPMAN PULLING EMERGENCY BRAKE ON

3

O'FARREL

GEARY

Fares please ... ting ting ... Let's go.

Not too fast ... and not too slow ...

Stop at the crossing ...

Wait for the light ...

POST

SUTTER

Then ride the cable

right up to the top ...

Stop ... and look at the view.

BUSH

PINE

DING A TI DING DING · DING DING

CALIFORNIA

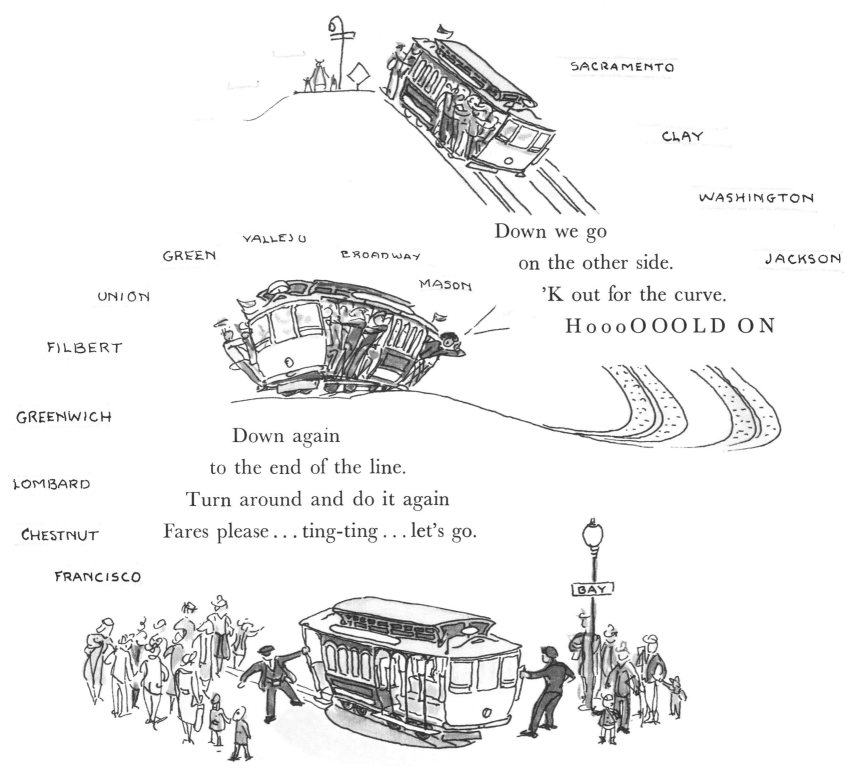

SACRAMENTO

CLAY

WASHINGTON

JACKSON

Down we go
on the other side.
'K out for the curve.
HoooOOOLD ON

GREEN   VALLEJO   BROADWAY

MASON

UNION

FILBERT

GREENWICH

Down again
to the end of the line.
Turn around and do it again
Fares please...ting-ting...let's go.

LOMBARD

CHESTNUT

FRANCISCO

BAY

No hill too steep . . .
no load too heavy . . .
Always cheerful . . .
and most polite . . .

She rang her gong
and sang her song
from early morn
till late at night.

6

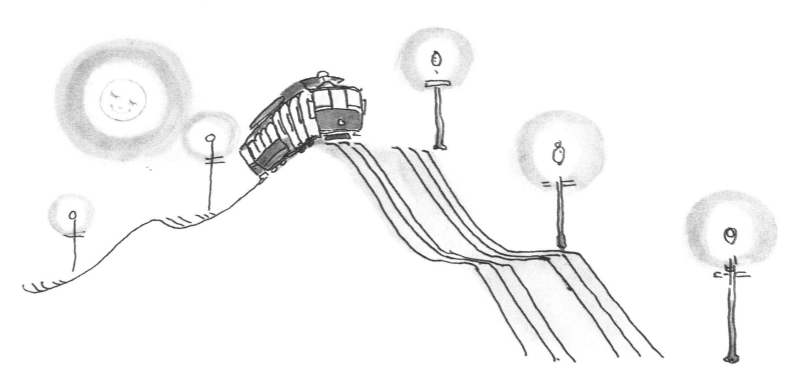

From late at night
to early morn...
Maybelle rested
with her sisters
in the big green barn.

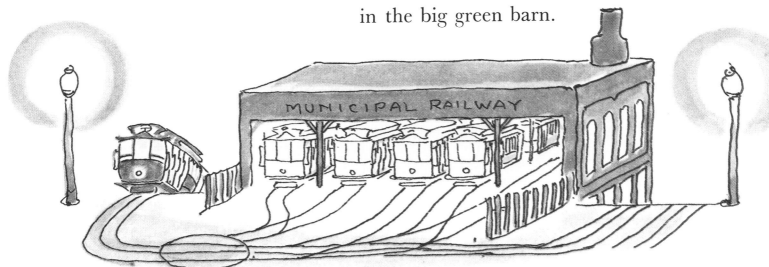

MUNICIPAL RAILWAY

7

Born in San Francisco long ago
they had watched their City change and grow,
the new come in and the old go out
while they remained the same.

At night while the City slept
they exchanged the news of the day
or played the game "Remember when..."
until it was time to go out again.

"Remember when the City was small
when everyone knew everyone else
and nobody hurried and nobody worried.
Those were the good old times.

"Remember when mansions crowned the hills
when our family was large and rich and famous,
the pride of the City and joy of the people.
Those were the gay old times.

"Remember the Sunday afternoon rides
out to the public parks and beaches
and the all-day outings on holidays.
Those were the merry old times."

They seldom remembered the terrible fire
which destroyed the City overnight.
Instead they remembered how quickly the City
rebuilt and grew some more.

They remembered when many of the cable lines
were changed into electric lines
and they remembered the first horseless carriage
and how people laughed and yelled "get a horse."

Now the streets were crowded with traffic
and everyone hurried and seemed to be worried.
Electric trolleys and gasoline buses had
replaced almost all of the old family lines.

Maybelle and her sisters worked for the City.
The City had been so busy growing
she had neglected her little cable cars
and they needed a new coat of paint.

Maybelle was always first out in the morning
and last to come in at night.
She loved her City . . . she loved her work
and most of all she loved the people.

MUNICIPAL RAILWAYS

Maybelle's hill was very steep

and very slippery when wet...

Even taxi cabs stayed off this hill

in damp or foggy weather...BUT

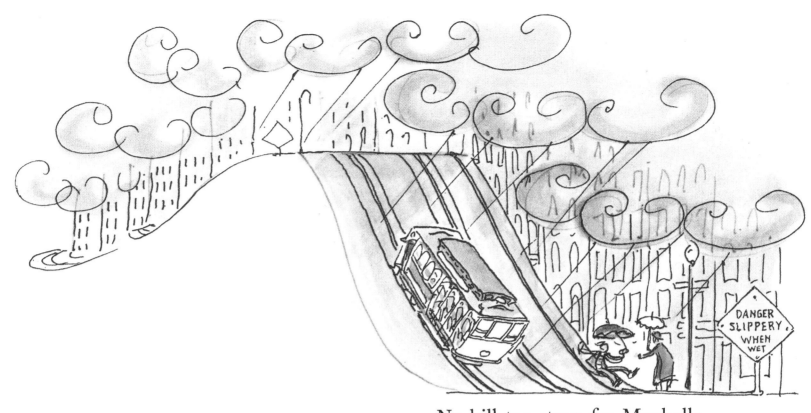

No hill too steep for Maybelle...
No matter the weather...wet or dry.
She could not slip...she had her grip
and three kinds of brakes besides.

TING! TING! TING!

17

When visitors came from the rest of the world
to see the sights of the City ... they admired
the beautiful views ... the two big bridges
the public buildings and parks and zoos
but what they liked the most of all
was to ride on a little cable car.

They paid no attention to the trolleys and buses
because they had plenty of those at home.

This made Big Bill, the bus,
   just a bit jealous.
      "After all," he boasted,
         "I'm bigger and stronger
            and newer and faster
               and more economical."

His route ran by the City Hall
   and he knew the City Fathers.

One day as Maybelle was going along
taking her time and singing her song
Big Bill honked his horn and hooted
"Out of my way . . . out of my way . . .
you little old cable car . . .
I just heard the City Fathers say
the cable cars must go . . .
that you're too old and out of date
much too slow and can't be safe . . .

and worst of all YOU DON'T MAKE MONEY.
What they want is Speed and Progress
and E-CON-O-MY . . . and that means US.
Ho ho . . . poor little old cable car . . .
Too bad you're not a bus,"
and he ground his gears
and shoved his way into traffic
leaving a trail of gasoline fumes
and Maybelle sad and unhappy.

"Oh me . . . oh my . . . oh dearie me . . .
If this is true what shall we do.
Anyway I'd rather be me . . .
a little old cable car
than a great big old . . .
clumsy old . . . stuffy old . . .
and yes . . . smelly old bus."
She said as she choked
on the gasoline fumes.

Of course she didn't say this out loud
because she was much too polite.

22

The rest of the day
seemed long and dreary
Maybelle's heart was
sad and weary...
The hills too high
the load too heavy
Her bell rang wrong.

DONG DING DING DONG

23

Soon the news leaked out from City Hall
what the City Fathers planned to do.

Some people said, "Too bad . . .
Hate to see them go . . . Progress, I suppose."
Others sighed and said, "We'll miss them . . . What a pity
for our City to lose her cable cars . . . We'll be like any city."
And one person said . . . "Why do we have to?
We, the people, are the City.
Why can't we decide?"

So they called a public meeting
in the Public Library
of all the friends of the cable cars
and called themselves

THE CITIZENS' COMMITTEE TO SAVE THE CABLE CARS.

Letters and telegrams
poured in from all over the world
begging the City Fathers to keep
the cable cars.

The Citizens' Committee stormed City Hall
demanding a chance for the people to vote,
to answer the question YES or NO,
SHALL THE CITY KEEP HER CABLE CARS?

"Pooh pooh,"
said the City Fathers,
"Just sentimental talk...besides
you need to have a petition
to put the question
on the ballot."

No sooner said than done.
The people signed a petition
and presented it to City Hall.

So the fate
of Maybelle and her sisters
was put on the ballot as Question One,
The Citizens' Committee got busy
with posters, parades
and publicity.

Every day there were speeches
and the people started taking sides.
Some said "YES", and some said "NO"
but nobody said perhaps or maybe.

The "No" people had facts and figures
and the "Yes" people answered with more.
The "No" people made more noise
but the "Yes" people worked harder.

Big Bill, the bus, was sure he'd win
so late at night while the City slept
he crept out to practice climbing
Maybelle's hill...up and down...
stop...and start...

"Nothing to it," boasted Bill,
"What's all the fuss about this hill?"

Then came one damp and foggy night
when Big Bill tried to stop half way down.
He slipped . . . he slid . . . he turned around.
"Whew, that was close," groaned Bill.
"I don't think I like this hill."

THE POLLS ARE OPEN

At last Election Day arrived
when the people would decide by vote
whether the cable cars would stay or go.
The polls opened at seven in the morning
and closed at eight at night.

THE POLLS ARE CLOSED

No more speeches . . . no more talking . . .
just one vote from each and everyone
and no one could tell what the answer
would be until the polls were closed
and all the votes counted.

The people stood around quietly and waited
for the votes to be counted...Maybelle waited...
Big Bill waited...the whole City waited
to see what the answer would be.

Nine o'clock . . . ten o'clock . . . eleven o'clock . . . midnight.

"Hurray," shouted the people. "The answer is YES.

The cable cars have won . . . three to one.

Hurray for the cable cars . . . Long may they live."

They gathered around Maybelle
and covered her with flowers.
They turned her around
and all climbed on.
"No fares please...
    Ting ting...let's go
        This ride's on me
            and free for all."

DING GA TI DING DING DING DING

It reminded Maybelle
of the "good old times"
when everyone knew
everyone else . . .
and life was gay
and friendly.

On her way back Maybelle met Big Bill.
"Congratulations," he honked, "I'm glad you won.
Your hill's too steep for me and
much too slippery when wet."
"Thank you," rang Maybelle,
"and let's be friends."

"Okay," said Bill, "and by the way
I just heard the new City Fathers say
that you and your sisters each would have
a new coat of paint...also they have named
one day each year to celebrate
as CABLE CAR DAY."

THANKYOU AGAIN..TING TING..AND GOODNIGHT

YOU'RE WELCOME..BEEP BEEP...BE SEEIN' YOU

Home went Maybelle...clingety clang...
Ringing her gong and singing her song.
Good news...ting ting...good news she sang
Our day's not done...it's just begun.